For my friends Enrico and Luca
D. C.

Thank you Fanny
V. P.

Also by Davide Cali

- *A Dad Who Measures Up (with Anna Laura Cantone)*
- *The Bear with the Sword (with Gianluca Foli)*
- *I Like Chocolate (with Evelyn Daviddi)*
- *Santa's Suit (with Eric Heliot)*
- *Piano Piano (with Eric Heliot)*
- *The Enemy (with Serge Bloch)*
- *What Is This Thing Called Love? (with Anna Laura Cantone)*

First English language edition published in Australia and New Zealand in 2012 by
Wilkins Farago Pty Ltd (ABN 14 081 592 770)
PO Box 78, Albert Park, Victoria, Australia

Teachers Notes and other resources: **www.wilkinsfarago.com.au**

© 2009, Editions Sarbacane, Paris
English language translation rights arranged through La Petite Agence, Paris.
English translation © 2012, Wilkins Farago Pty Ltd

Wilkins Farago would like to thank Elsa Klockenbring and Philippine McDonald for their assistance with the English translation for this book.
Printed by Everbest Printing, China
Distributed by Dennis Jones & Associates (Australia & NZ)

10 LITTLE insects

Davide Cali Vincent Pianina

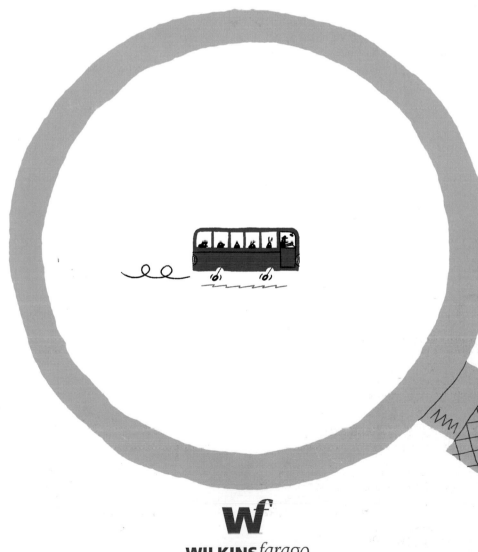

wf
WILKINS *farago*

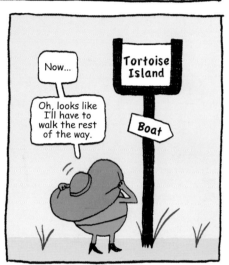

2

4

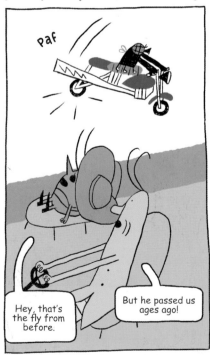

6

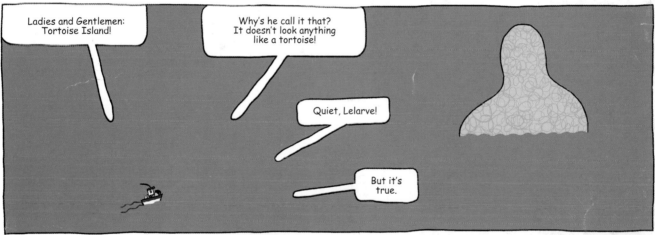

Where's the lift?

FLAP FLAP

The Nobel Prize for Medicine ...

The Marathon Gold medal ...

Country Song of the Year ...

The Best Stick in the Universe ...

I can't take anymore. How many stairs do you think we have climbed?

Aha!

Only a few steps left.

Phew!

Aaah!

Finally!

About time.

What a bunch of wimps. I could have climbed for another hour.

It's enormous!

Yes, not bad.

A bit over the top, perhaps ...

Indeed.

Hopefully dinner is also over the top. I'm starving.

Ladies and Gentlemen, dinner is served.

Give me a big serve. I haven't had lunch today.

But?! It looks like ...

...dung!

It's not bad, eh?

Excuse me, what else is there?

Nothing.

Yuck! This is disgusting.

Who do you think we are?

Pass over your plates!

Same here!

12

This is all a bit strange.

Yes.

I've got a feeling this medical conference will never take place.

Relax, guys.
I'm going to play one of my songs instead.

bleng

Oh my dear Oklahoma!!

Ooooooh ...

What do you think of all this?

I prefer the blues.

... my dear

Oklahomaa!

No, I meant the fact that everyone received a different invitation?

And that's it.

Bravo!

Want another one?

Don't trouble yourself ...

... I've found a record player!

1
4

Good evening, my dear victims!!

If you hear this message ...

know that within two days

you're going to pay for your misdeeds!

You're all going to die!

Oops!

Ha! Ha! Ha! Ha! Ha! Ha! Ha! Ha! Ha!

What's that all about?

I don't know, it was here before we arrived!

I prefer country music.

Frankly, it's a joke in bad taste.

I agree.

What's on the other side?

"You're all going to die (instrumental version)".

1
5

That's impossible! We all drank the wine.

So his glass was the only one with poison in it!

The butler must be the murderer!

Wait a minute, how can you say that?

But look ...

But it's always the butler, isn't it?

Only in crime novels!

You can only accuse him of serving wine that's a bit tasteless.

This story reminds me of a movie ...

It took place in a house where the ten guests dropped like flies, one after the other ...

It was a novel by Agatha Christie originally, lad.

A classic detective story.

But that's very different from us, my friends. In the novel, they were all guilty of something.

I'm guilty of something ...

Once, I took drugs before taking part in a marathon.

I must confess my beautiful skin tone isn't natural: I use green makeup!

Okay, I have something serious to confess!

Once, during an impressionist competition ...

... I needed to go to the toilet.

So, I put a stick on my seat so no one would steal it.

Then I went ...

... and when I returned, the judge was in front of my seat.

He thought the stick was me!

He gave me first prize and I didn't say anything.

Ever since, I've been famous for my stick impression.

I did worse. One day, I farted and accused the stinkbug next to me. I ruined her reputation!

I'm always putting my feet into cake icing.

That's nothing! I'm a murderer!

When I was a young doctor, I wanted to heal an injured millipede.

As I couldn't sew him up, I thought I would cut him in half, so that each part could live separately.

A horrible mistake. It's worms that can be cut in two, not millipedes. My patient died.

You're not a murderer, you're just a bad doctor.

I've also had victims in my work, but never on purpose.

What about that squashed silkmoth you told me about?

As I said: never on purpose.

What about the hanged scarab beetle?

Same thing.

What about the cricket that was burned to a crisp?

and the m ...

What about you – nothing to confess?

Cheeky little rascal.

No, I'm only a three-week-old larva and I haven't had time to do anything yet.

There's someone else who's more than three weeks old who hasn't talked yet ...

Me? I've never done anything bad. Apart from tearing off my husband's head before eating him.

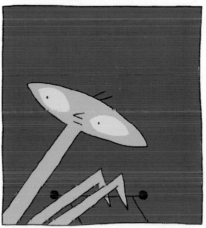

But that's normal for a praying mantis!

2
1

Saturday

Ah! Looks like it's going to be a great day.

Aaaarghi!!...

Maybe I spoke too soon ...

I heard someone screaming!

It was me ...

Come!

I was about to get something from the deep freeze, and this is what I found ...

Mrs Mantis !!!

That's got nothing to do with it!!

Make no mistake, he's the one who poisoned Krikkit and froze the maid and cut the telephone line and, on top of that he has the keys to all the rooms, including McFly's!

Stop! You're jumping to conclusions.

Gracey knew Mr Krikkit was allergic... but she didn't touch the cider bottle in the kitchen.

The butler added cider to the wine, but he knew nothing of the allergy.

Gracey suggested Longshanks cross the lake,

But it was the doctor and me who went with him and encouraged him.

Anyone could have put glue on McFly, broken the handle in the deep freeze and cut the phone line.

We've got no proof!

And who's to say that the murderer is one of us?

Not bad.

Okay, off I go!

Let's cheer him on.

WOOHOO!

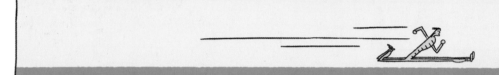

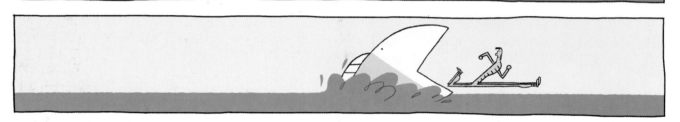

GLOUP !

No doubt about it.

That was a record of sorts.

For God's sake!

He's died stuck to a sheet of paper!

Who'd be cruel enough to put a piece of fly paper in a fly's bedroom?

No, this isn't fly paper.

Oh look, an unfinished model motorbike ...

McFly probably wanted to finish it ...

... but got some glue on his feet.

He must have picked up the piece of paper to wipe off the glue but the glue dried.

So he struggled ...

... got glue everywhere ...

... and died.

Who'd be cruel enough to put a model motorbike in a fly's bedroom?

You're right about one thing, the dead bodies are real.

But there is nothing to say it isn't a game.

The murderer is someone on the island.

And this maniac is keeping watch over his victims.

I suggest we play his game.

Let's set up search parties to find him!

How are we going to choose them?

I don't know. How about 'Eeny, meeny, miny, moe'?

Let's go.

Johnny Nail and the Doc, you explore the forest.

Caros and Gracey, search the mansion.

Duchateau, Lelarve and myself will search the cliffs.

Let's meet back here
in no more than thirty minutes.

Ok. Ok. Ok. Ok. Ok. Ok.

Go!

36

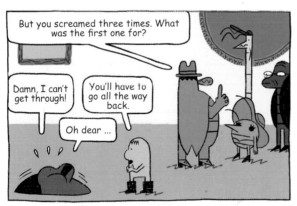

Without thinking, I pushed the nose of this dog and ...

CLICK!

Schwing!

I ...

I didn't do that on purpose!

I guess there'll be no-one to serve dinner tonight now.

He wasn't a real butler anyway.

Gnnnn!

Yes, but since we've been here, we keep on skipping meals!

And you're skinny enough!

Gnnnnnnnnnn!

Can't we swap?

We had an argument before he died, but we had just made up.

Tell me more!

Honestly! We even searched the mansion and came across a lighthouse at the top of the staircase!

A lighthouse!

Yes! We tried to get it working but it was broken.

What a pity!

Yes!

I've heard a thing or two about lighthouses ...

My father was a sailor. Perhaps I could have a look?

Crack!

A power cut in a storm. I might have known!

Let's see if there are any candles ...

That's a bit grim, isn't it?

It's the only one I could find.

47

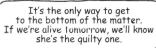

Hey!
What are you doing?
Open this door!

BANG
BANG

Sorry, madam, but it's been locked for your own safety.

Open up!

Are you sure this is a good idea?

BANG
BANG

It's the only way to get to the bottom of the matter. If we're alive tomorrow, we'll know she's the guilty one.

Goodnight!

You too!

Fancy another game of cards tomorrow?

Click!

Oh no!

Tonight, you sleep in your own bed!

Tweet Tweet Tweet
Tweet
Tweet

Ah! It's stopped raining!
Let's hope the boat comes today.

Tweet
Tweet
Tweet

How are you, Doc?

Still alive, what about you?

Clearly, the killer behaved himself last night.

Even so, I'm going to make sure Gracey is okay.

You never know ...

Ahem ...

SMACK!

About time! You're seriously beginning to annoy me!

Calm down!

You're kidding! You locked me up just because I killed Ceros, something that anyone could have done!

I agree, Ceros' death was an accident.

Aha!

5
3

But why would they do such a thing?

Scratch
Scratch

To make the murderer believe the Doctor was dead ...

... so the Doc could remain hidden and search for him without being a target.

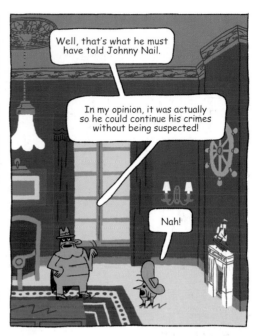

Well, that's what he must have told Johnny Nail.

In my opinion, it was actually so he could continue his crimes without being suspected!

Nah!

You're so far from the truth!

Doctor!

AAAAH!

Don't come near us!

Actually, I hid so I could find the murderer.

And now it's clear: there is no murderer on this island.

Oh yes? And just by chance, your accomplice has just died!

59

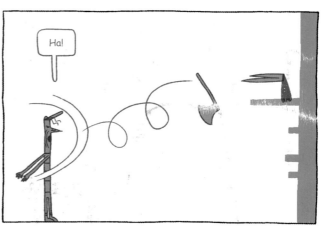

6
1

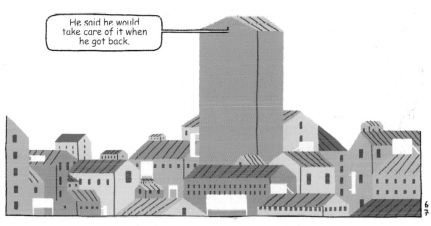

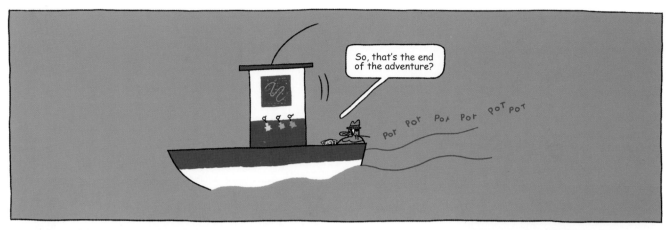

Davide Cali and Vincent Pianina.